Telegraph to the Sky

Telegraph to the Sky

Sandile Dikeni

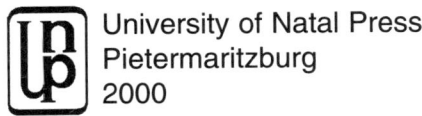

University of Natal Press
Pietermaritzburg
2000

Published by University of Natal Press
Private Bag X01, Scottsville 3209
South Africa

© Sandile Dikeni 2000

ISBN: 0 86980 978 4

The publisher is grateful to Mayibuye Books for permission to reprint the following
poems from *Guava Juice* (1992): Love poem for my country, Culture and Once again
on the altar for humanity.

Cover photograph by Oscar Gutierrez
Cover design by Brett Armstrong
Layout by Lesley Lewis, Inkspots, Durban
Printed by Interpak Books, Pietermaritzburg

For my wife, Bronia

Contents

Telegraph to the sky

Stay with me
when the sun rises
from a western sky
with silver spears lashing
at earth and our youth
when the eastern horizon
hangs smoke
as celebration to a fading dream
will you take my blistered hand
to a kiss?
That journey
between reflex action
and conviction
where moments flash
from substance to emotion
and where we count seconds as instinct
we live in times where we are against time
and impulse rules over us
as undirected, unelected factor
we live cliché as fact
and fact is cliché
to the one beat of change.

Will you stay with me
when I have no more hallelujahs
to your name
and instead offer dahlias
to your anonymity
when my knees refuse to bend at your beauty
but my eye of growth
raises an altar to your soul

that power that dreams awake
the Brazilian forest
or in its strength of wish
re-awakens our dead
at Kassinga, Biafra
or wherever your heart lives
among the innocent dead.
Will you really
stay with me
when I stand up
and sing to the world
its magnitude
its greatness
for an ability to turn itself
upside down
while the inhabitants still believe
in its constance

Unaware
that their heads are facing downwards.

Nowadays
they don't hang you by the neck
till you die.
They dangle you by the feet
till the blood comes to the brain.
It's a high feeling that makes you reach for sky
but touch earth as limit
as ecstacy
of reaching some end
because some journeys are so long
and much longer
when you live in a dream forest
called poetry.

They say
it is not by bread alone that we live.
I know.
It is by poetry alone that we survived –
with poetry dancing on our tongues
we wiped the blood from our mouths
we charmed our torturers
we dangled freedom bells from our shackles
we made music out of sirens
we made homes out of prisons
we redesigned parliaments out of corrugated iron
we petrol bombed our angry past
we blasted our martyrs out of our brains
and we made shrines out of their graves
we weaved forgiveness onto our T-shirts
and with last remaining droplets of blood
we tried to paint peace on angry dark skies
we silenced our solitude
we mated our humility with our anger
with hammers and chissels
we punched hope deep into our hearts
we swam, we danced and we played water games in our tears
and now,
now we wave flags so bright
sometimes brighter than our future
but stay with me.

Stay with me
when the jungle has no tree
when the wind has no breath
when the rain has no sea
the desert has no sand
the stars have no eyes to see
God has no mercy
and the devil is making barbecue out of the land.
Now, will you stay with me?

Stay, so that we sing
songs from experience
we sing ideas from consciousness
and let's cultivate destiny
from the barrenness of this,
this history.
Stay with me.

Shall you?

Please?

Way back home

One day,
someday,
should some Freedom be registered and final
Do not scoff, when I spit at the fruits of freedom
because maybe, my bongo
has the sound of a wail
and my voice, the anger of distance
and my movements
the estrangement of discontent
do not be angry

Do not be angry
when I can not recall that samba from Brazil
or if the Mozambican nights of celebration
help the nightmares in my red
do not be angry

Some claim
in some April
some freedom threatened and came
But Hitler was born in April
and Lenin celebrates life in April
and so do I
but what are the boundaries?
Rosa Luxemburg once asked
and I wonder
the questions of a Namibian poet
How far is Washington from Pretoria?
And how near Bonn to Tokyo?
Therefore
What is the mileage between hunger and wealth

what is the distance between the contentment
of nation
and the discontent of a continent
how much of a black comedy, really,
is Africa, to the unity of nations?
How satisfying are potatoes as a relief measure
dished out from gun greased hands
Italy loves Somalia
this much we know
from Benito Mussolini
And Michael Jackson loves Zairean children
across the diaspora
How much love do we need to get serious?

Maybe
if we do a tango in Lederhosen
and karate seven time a day
the G-Seven will give us G-Strings
to enter Hollywood
The most exciting act
since Zionists put Palestinians on the altar
and if we eat pasta
we will discover, the distance between
Italy and China is
as fragile as the love between
Great Britain and Northern Ireland
The lofty ideas of the Eiffeltower
are as crazy
as the time bomb mentality in Big Ben,
as crazy
as the love between Napoleon and Nelson
How far a laugh is Mandela from X?
and before Y and Z seal us,
shall we not rather
ask the spirit of the Ghaza

to be our blood
and the blood of the Sioux and the Maya
to be our spirit?
So that we drum it in the drums of Uhuru
when it bangs in the pangs
of a continent
Che might be dead,
but was his chair only in Cuba?
So, why do you wonder
when my freedom
only sings me an Internationale
because maybe,
just maybe,
that,
this,
is my distance from home.

Reasoning

the reasoning of history dangles
unsatisfied at the dawn
of new words
attempting to quest the minds
of millions and millions
of miserable souls
wandering in the meadows of confusion
words must live
in the daily ambits of practise
the scourges of the past are removed
only when you wipe the bloodstains
that flood the memory
No amount of intention
even good, honest and earnest
can mystify the racist murder
that fertilised the soil of uprising
no goodwill is enough to dry the tears
of centuries that flow
in the rivers of sorrow.
Not even lies written in contempt
can remove the contempt
templed in the abyss of remembrance
that spells the tendencies of hatred and vengeance
as manufactured and brewed in the tombs of torture
someone,
you, must clean the cellar casks
of ignorance and deprivation.
Shout it out
for the graves to open their ears.

Confess to kwashiorkor and malaria
deflate the inflated arms of destruction
destroy the thrones of racist felony
to be trodden down by the facts of history,
so that nations and worlds might learn
that nazis and murderers are still alive
engraved in the bitter memories of divided nations.
Unifications in wealth
deny the wealth of wisdom
embedded in the true sweat of labour

Wet dreams on the G7 feeding

When the G7 feeds
it prefers a Sumo size table.
It feeds on Sushi,
they take it delicately,
the way one would hold a yen.

The G7 can pump itself with weisswurst ...
schnell in and out of the mouth.
The G7 gets an erection.
The D-Mark pretends it's a G7-Mark stands up in a goose step pose.
Salutes.

The G7 worms down kilometres of pasta
drowns it in red wine.
Somalians with no table manners
and with stiletto tongues say,
"Red wine and pasta look like blood and worms."

The G7 dines on invisible morsels
smaller than their canines.
They cover their Apres Rasage mouths.
Frankly speaking, they should not be seen
feeding in the fashion of Frankensteins like Bokassa.

The G7 also feeds on pounds of Yorkshire pudding,
and pukes immediately.
This, they say, is not a reflection on the English economy!

The G7 cuts deep into buffalo flesh.
And when the natives chant "death to the enemy"
The G7 claps, comments, "How wild. How exotic!"

The G7 yanks and forces down large hamburgers.
They wonder how McDonald's does it
... they at least know about Coke in Cocaine.

And while the G7 feeds
the (s)cented parts of my country dream badly of a G8
only, nobody knows if:
Boerewors, braaivleis, pap
and the limbs of the workers will qualify as cuisine.

New ways of running the world (the green way)

i ran from Auschwitz.

i ran with gas fumes clogging the aorta in the lungs.

i ran through Hiroshima to Nagasaki collecting shrapnel for the brain.

i ran into Vietnam with the hand of Von Guyab in my hand and barbed wire forced into ear through ear.

i ran into Managua, for electric manacles on the testicles.

i ran into Santiago with a Chilean child in my heart and the shining path in her eyes.

i ran into Dublin. the bells were tolling far and fast as i ran.

i ran into Ghaza with stones in my hands and bullets in my heart.

i limped into Oshakati hop-skipping limpet mines.

i ran the red soil of Soweto with a burning tyre around my neck.

one day i wish to stop for a moment.
not to rule and run the world!
but to kiss the earth
that kiss caressed my feet
while i ran.

Short changed

How we change
our tongues
sweet drooping the flavour
of guava juices
from love point of view
and whispering
in nights filled with committee meetings
awu, comrade woman
will you take me into hiding tonight?
or others masturbating with
copies of Rosa Luxemburg
sighing, "The nation state, oh the nation state"
and everything blurring
to the absolute smell of burning
tyres and desires

How we change
our words are stenched with cool coca cola's
rapped from love angle
and shouting from
above the trials of OJ Simpson
Yo, Baby, Yo
let me sex you up tonight
and holy other going up high with copies of madonna
undressing the virgin
keeping the rubber nearby
eyes shut, in fear of Aids
and heaven comes smelling like
Chanel or banal

Mozambique

There is nothing here
only drunken words
stumbling and burping
over commas,
crashing into syntaxes
and precariously hanging
        around

cliff-
faced
fullstops.

There is some void
wiping our faces
and voices
the hand of a blind groping for solid
in that darkness
        around

darkness.

There is patriotism
dark suited in deja-vu
performing
the limp dicked
dance
        around

vague possibilities.

But wait ...
there are people here
peoplepeoplepeoplepeople
so beautiful and complex

like my doctor's handwriting.

Letter from Jerusalem

to my mum

Mama,
here,
little David
does not play his harp
he makes music on an Uzi
he does not carry any sling
there is no Goliath,
only children from the Intifada
throwing stones at David and the walls
of history.

12.01.1997

Goodbye England

When they killed Sipho
Mrs Jones was furious

They killed him at four o'clock
in the afternoon
and she could taste his blood
in her afternoon tea

A long story

My comrades and friends killed my granny
with fire ...
But before that, they sucked her breasts dry
... so that she could burn well

London: 26.09.95

May Day

Today,
with more than servitude,
humble and filled with pride,
i surrender my thanks and loyalty,
even my body and dignity,
into these safe but brutalised hands

hands that carried the brutal land,
hands that rocked the precious land,
until it calmly breathed
this day
the workers' day
Take this day
from it you shall weave
better days
even the future so brittle and shaky
shall be cemented and plastered
shall be spannered and tightened
to certainty and security
in the hands of the workers
i surrender this day
may the sun shine

Love poem for my country

My country is for love
so say its valleys
where ancient rivers flow
the full circle of life
under the proud eye of birds
adorning the sky

My country is for peace
so says the veld
where reptiles caress
its surface
with elegant motions
glittering in their pride

My country
is for joy
so talk the mountains
with baboons
hopping from boulder to boulder
in the majestic delight
of cliffs and peaks

My country
is for health and wealth
see the blue of the sea
and beneath
the jewels of fish
deep under the bowels of soil
hear
the golden voice
of a miner's praise
for my country

My country
is for unity
feel the millions
see their passion
their hands are joined together
there is hope in their eyes

we shall celebrate

Love letter

Another sun
has kissed blessing
on my forehead
and i would smile
at nature's beauty

but
i miss your laughter's tapestry
so now i climb the wings of distance
to sing in your heart
a serenade
come,
let's walk the garden

The Spirit of Mojo

Brother, you say
This thing disrupted lives
You say
I say how?

Someone killed the blue note in mid feeling
in some blue sensed district
where, they say
perfect timing was saxed up and down
the seven steps
of a jazzy dance
and the blue life
of one passionate moment in freedom
when knife
wielding dreamers
soaked abandoned anger
in a breathless chord
so they say, today
in mellow tones
and Mannenberg breathes
through wounds
a careful C-flat
for the Cape Flats
where life is sometimes
simply fat
or flat depending on the ABCDE or F's
of our musical lives.

A madala told me,
when they raped Sophia,
the sound
he nearly blew himself away
others jazz stepped away
running naked but horny
humming a thrust as entry into exile
others bluesy but birdy
as ntyilo-ntyilo, song of the bird
and others in slapping shame hid
behind cultural curtains
praying for rain
to fall on beautiful Sophia
woman of many talents
and now you know
there is no triumph in this thing.

I heard from a dancing snake
that in the land of the spear
the whistle of a bamboo flute was pierced
two ways:
Zulu and Indian
and not even the call of Satyagraha
not even the determination of Shaka
let alone the sweet whistle of sugar cane
could deflavour the salty water
from brow or eye
in the sugar plantations.
There we still spit blues
bitter as the Indian Ocean
but still give me the song
I like the chilli in my mealie.

Dreamers do not know
that: Johny Dyani
Dudu Pukwana
Chris McGregor
and Mongezi Feza
blew and bassed their final notes
dreamers only know
that: Dollar Brand
Bheki Mseleku
and Hugh Masakela
are still alive
in a music stance called African Jazz
We are all still alive
in the spirit of Mojo.

Lean Blues

fat woman singing
lean blues
and the rain pouring
from happy heaven
and a dream killer folds his hands
either stupefied or dream captured
by a fat rainbow
calling from the bowels
of a big woman's heart

fat blues hopping
from a tiny woman's voice
and turquoise sky
shooting emeralds
and a dream hunter sighs
either tired
or deflated
a step away from the pot of gold
in the rainbow strings
of a small woman's heart

Lesego

How come they make bombs out of words and dreads?

Township boy

as a boy
i murdered Jack Horner
took him out of his corner,
out of the school yard
into a culvert
licked him
and chowed his christmas pie

Wee Willy Winkie
i chased with a knife
(an Okapi)
took away his night gown and candle
for my mom
and told him:
"it's past eight o'clock"

Mary had a little lamb
until i slew it
and cooked it
but someone stole it
out of my pot
it was the boy who hangs down the lane

Small things

it's small things
that make children laugh
it's a grain of curry in your eye
another drop in your sneeze
it's a bright flag whipping the wind

but mostly
it's the laughter in your laugh
that makes children laugh

Biko

The man is not dead
he's in Parliament.
He punctuates the words
of Parliamentarians
with his breath,
his black fingers
peruse the white paper
sentence to sentence
sense from nonsense

Biko's gone corporate
he shakes his head
from proposal to proposal
he's developed
a disapproval to "developments"

Biko is on stage
he sings with Sting
he dances with those who dance
alone

Biko's black fist
clasps hammers
with rhythmic strokes
like a heartbeat
he punches nails
into the obstinate souls of amnesiacs

Biko is only building another shack
at this moment
Biko is at a brothel.
he watches black man
nailing white woman
and white man
nailing black woman
they talk a lot when they are on top
they call it shagging
Biko says:
that's not what I meant

Biko goes to a shebeen
he sips a beer
but mostly he listens
drinks his own words
from the drunkard's mouth
and he gets dizzy
he writes what he likes
in freestyle

Biko directs traffic
it's an affirmative action job
he hates it but he does it
on behalf of women,
gays
cripples
blacks
latino's
natives
in that order of disgust
that rules the ruler's heart.
That's why he does it from the heart?

Biko hates doing movies
he enters production house
leaving without producing
frustrated,
I think Biko is an egoist
he thinks his will can not be done
I think it could,
at gun point

Biko is sometimes a pacifist
an ambidexterous schizophrene
he does stupid things
right hand
in the mouth of a tank in Rwanda
left hand
in the hand of an illegal immigrant
Biko walks across borders
strolls over landmines
and the minds
of intellectuals
without a visa

Biko attends funerals
he hugs widows
puts sand in the widower's hand
grabs a spade and cries like all of us
like an ordinary orphan
there are two ways of looking
the man is dead
or
the man is not dead

Thoughts on a poet hanging

for Ken Saro Wiwa

"blood is thicker than oil" – Chirikure Chirikure

When the fat arsed belly of the tyrant's dream gasps for oil
it lubricates its greedy paws in a poet's blood

Few know this:

When poets hang
their words dangle in the air
tight like a hangman's rope
above a tyrant's head

When poets hang
their words drip
like blood
from dead lips
and drop
into the tyrant's greasy oil cup

Track of the tracks

for my brother Dicey, who died of TB at the Railways

It begins with a laugh
hard and breathless
as steel:
Xhegwazana pheki'papa
Xhegwazana pheki'papa
sayithath'apha
sayibek'apha
sayithath'apha
sayibek'apha
My mama makes porridge
my granny makes porridge
my mama makes porridge
my granny makes porridge
Take it here
put it there
take it here
put it there
There
the night comes
sweating
perspiring outwards
drags the guts
in a blood red pull
that drains sweat
of youth
out
out to the harshness of world
that leaves you cold
cold when sun unveils
generous blanket of light
that never touches the inside

and bone and marrow shrivel
ice
stone
inside, outside
inside the railways tracks
where we chant:
Sojikel'emaweni
emaweni,
Sojikel'emaweni
sojikela phi na he?
he wena
sojikela phi na he
he wena
We bend the cliffs
the cliffs
we bend the cliffs
the cliffs
we bend them for you
and you
hey you!
Our breath is hot
like the hiss of Makadas the steam train
that puffs against the winter wall of a Karoo drought
and bends and swerves
through our lives
dark and black
as the soot at the coal mines
of Newcastle
where some more black blood coughs
from deep down:
Sishov'ingolovane
ngolovane
Sishov'ingolovane
ngolovane

We push the small coal trains
against a Winter's white breath
that cracks under our boots,
melts into ice crystals
and still we shall sing
warm longings:
Sdudla sibomvu
mathangan'abomvu
Sdudla sibomvu
mathangana'abomvu
sing, sing
until death comes
sings in our breath

Culture

White theatres
overflow with the drama:
TO BE OR NOT TO BE.

Black townships
are drained by the drama:
TB OR NOT TB.

Once again on the altar for humanity

deep down in the past
the survivors were fit
to roam and conquer
to achieve and progress
when the wailing winds
fought against the will
and the rain
mingled with their tears
and the mighty seas
salted their wounds
deep down in centuries
they fought against the years
hard and battled in experience
they celebrated
victories over days
tense and untamed
they tamed themselves
into soft components of the universe
they harmonised
the precarious tomorrows
that came with the sun
and left with the sun
and went with men and women
as it dived into horizons
of long long ago
moons ago
under the kiss of the moon
they strengthened their vows
to pledge their survival
in moons, suns, rains, and seas to come

today
hesitant under the glittering stars
shall they falter
to place themselves
once again on the altar?